Adventures of

BAD CRAB

It took a bit of sweat ...
and months and months
of convincing.

But finally, we headed to the store. Surprised to find pets and pets galore.

The landlord said
NO DOGS ALLOWED.
She said they are worse
than a big crowd.

A fish in dish?
Who can play with a fish?

A frog who eats flies?
I do not advise!

Have you heard
"If it's free it's for me."
Well, a crab with
a fancy shell
... now that sounded
just swell.

Home with me this little crab went ...
Along with a new cage and his colorful tent.

A great adventure
had begun. We were both
ready to have some fun.

First a name.
Not just any old
name. One that
would give him much
deserved fame.

I knew his name would just appear. But, I didn't know he was mischievous and had no fear.

My crab and
I weren't on
the same page.
Quite frankly
stated, he
didn't care for
a cage.

When I was
tucked in tight,
when my mom
had turned off
all the light.

My crab headed to
the floor. And next he
headed out the door.

My crab made the great escape!
Then he tangoed
with a roll of tape.

My crab found a mid-night snack,

Would you believe he didn't put the milk back?

He sat on the couch
to watch TV.
He helped himself
to a cup of tea.

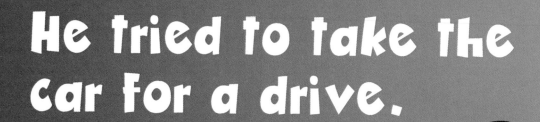

He tried to take the car for a drive.

I found him there
at a quarter to five.

He was fast
asleep by 5:03.

Zzz!

But the next time
I saw him, he was
in a tree.

A trip to the attic to explore ... We saw his claw prints in the dust on floor. Getting up there must have been a chore.

The adventures of my crab continue. The vacuum had become an issue.

Once we found him
in the garbage disposal.
I swear his grin was
almost boastful.

He made friends with Chomps, the dog. Together they got lost in the fog.

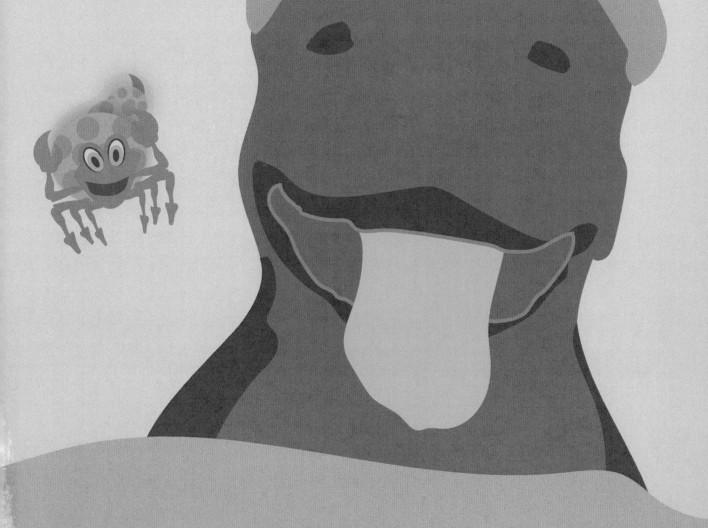

He played in the sandbox
with Cupcake the cat.
He even dawned a big
sun hat.

We chased him down the street when he tried to fly a kite. That time my crab had quite the fright.

The adventures of
my crab just never end.
And so, his name
we did amend

A nick name maybe, that he could embrace. Something to shout when he's running a race.

The adventures of my
crab became ... a way for
us to find his name.

Bad Crab was bad,
and that was true.

But his nickname fit
as nicknames do.

Do you have a nickname?

Why does your nickname fit you?

What mischief can
Bad Crab get into with
you? Take a photo
with your Bad Crab
and have a grown up
post it with the
#adventuresofbadcrab

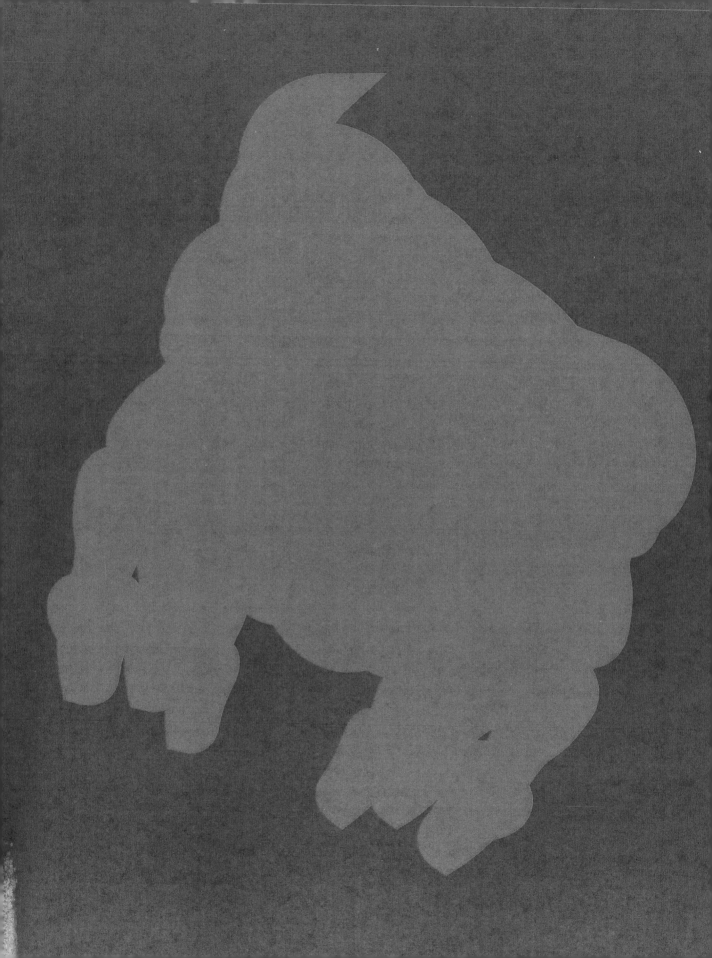